The Little Penguin

Written by A. J. Wood
Illustrated by Stephanie Boey

D1123912

PIPPBROOK BOOKS

Far away in a land where there is only ice and snow, Big Penguin sat feeling hungry and cold. He looked down at his feet. There, beneath the warm fold of his tummy, was an egg.

His egg.

He had been waiting for it to hatch for a very long time.

"Come on, Little Penguin," he said.

Days passed. Suddenly, a noise broke the snowy silence – a CRACK and a peep-peep-peep! Little Penguin had hatched.

'At last,' thought Big Penguin, looking proudly down at his chick. Little Penguin was covered in tiny, soft feathers as gray as the mist that sometimes rolled in off the faraway sea.

"One day you will be an Emperor of the Ice like me," his father told him and Little Penguin felt excited and proud all at the same time.

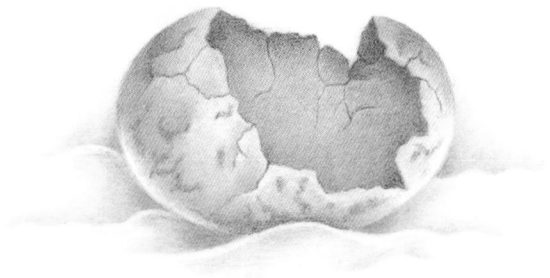

Big Penguin carried Little Penguin on his feet to a place where many penguins had gathered.

There were Adelies and Chinstraps, Gentoos and Rockhoppers, and great Emperor penguins just like Little Penguin's father.

Little Penguin looked up at the big penguins with their sleek, shiny feathers and their long, strong beaks and wished more than anything for the day when he could look like them.

There were little penguins too, lots of them – in a great gray huddle on the ice. "We will be safe and warm here tonight," said Big Penguin. "But tomorrow we must set off for the faraway sea, to find your Mother and swim in the deep waters of the ocean. You must remember to stay close, Little Penguin, for it is cold and lonely out on the big ice plain. It is easy to get lost."

But Little Penguin wasn't listening. He was too excited by the thought of the sea and what he would find there.

The next day the penguins set off on their journey. Little Penguin stuck close to his father at first but as the day wore on, he began to grow bored. Ahead was a great bank of snow with a strange creature sitting on top.

"I wonder what that can be?"

said Little Penguin, and he went to take a look.

It was a huge bird, bigger even than Big Penguin. The bird looked at Little Penguin with a beady eye.

"And who are you?" asked the bird.

"I am Little Penguin, and one day I will be an Emperor of the Ice like my father."

"That seems very unlikely," said the bird. "Especially as your feathers are falling out!"

Little Penguin looked down in dismay. Sure enough great clumps of his soft, gray feathers had fallen out and were lying on the snow.

Then, night fell. In the distance Little Penguin saw moonlight glinting where the great plain of ice gave way to the sea. He hurried on, shedding feathers as he went. Suddenly, two penguins came hurrying towards him. It was his mother and father.

"Where have you been Little Penguin?" they cried. "We have been waiting for you to swim with us in the blue waters of the ocean. Come!"

Little Penguin was so excited that he forgot all about his falling-out feathers and jumped with his parents into a magical underwater world...

"Will I freeze without my feathers?" Little Penguin asked his mother when they were sitting back upon the ice.
"But you have beautiful feathers," exclaimed his mother.
"Look!"

And when Little Penguin gazed at his reflection in the blue water he saw that it was true. His soft, gray feathers had all gone, but new ones had grown in their place—sleek and shiny feathers, just like his father's.

"Now you too are an Emperor of the Ice," said Big Penguin. And Little Penguin was excited and proud all at the same time for at last he knew it was true.